Princess Sovii

ISBN: 978-0-578-28310-4

First printing edition 2022 in the United States.

Princess Sovii

by

Brittany Sconiers

Illustrated by

Pratteek Das

This is Princess Sovii!
Sweet like a candy.
Giggly like a baby.

But when it comes to life's
muddles and puddles
Princess Sovii is strong like a lady.

Princess Sovii is the girl
with the curls,
And twisty-turny twirls.

She's bold and witty,
And she likes to wear pearls!

She likes her cookies crunchy,
Her ice cream chunky
Her chocolate cake spongy
And her hair in a scrunchie.

She speaks the truth.
Even when it's not pretty!

She's the bravest girl we know,
Though she's quite itty-bitty.

She likes to dress-up early in the day.
She looks royal in her princessy way

She's a smart thinker,
She's got thoughts in her head.
She loves to read books,
And she's quite well-read!

If she has an opinion,
She'd like you to know.

She's a fabulous little girl,
Her Papa thinks so!

When on the playground,
She's the wittiest girl around.

Her funny baby jokes,
Will have you rolling on the ground!

But there are days
When things don't go her way.

She stumbles and tumbles,
And walks with a sway.

Those days she holds on
To her family and friends.

'Cause she knows
what her Mama says,
"Love wins in the end!"

So, she sits with her friends,
Playing games in the sand.

When a fight breaks out,
All stare wide-eyed.

Kai and Sohai
are huffing and puffing.
Facing-off on opposite sides!

He took my tea cup!" says Sohai.
"She took my ball!" says Kai.

"No fights here," says Princess Sovii.
"Let's be kind to each other."

Kai and Sohai do not agree.
"We don't want to play together!"

Let's hear each other out,"
says Princess Sovii.
"We won't solve the problem
if you scream and shout."

So, they huddle together
on the sand.
And they hold onto
each other's hand.

"I want to play with the teacup," says Kai.
"I want to play with the ball," says Sohai.

Then Princess Sovii asks,
"Why don't you share?"

Kai and Sohai frown and scowl.
"But that's not fair!"

"But friends always share,"
says Princess Sovii.
"It's how we show we care"

"Don't you care?" she asks.
"If you do, you'd share."

So, they do.
And oh, what fun it is!

It's even better!
Playing together like this!

And the next stop for Princess Sovii
Is home sweet home.

Where she likes to cuddle,
With Mama, Papa and her sisters.

Telling each other stories
And talking in whispers.

In the life of Princess Sovii,
Every day is an adventure!

But with her head held high
And her dark eyes bright,
Princess Sovii strives every day
To do only what is right!

Brittany Sconiers borned and raised in Nashville, TN. She gained a passion to write children's books because she didn't enjoy reading as a child. Growing up, she felt that reading was boring. So, she decided to make sure that other children didn't feel the way she did by writing children's books that are fun to read.

Her book ideas come from wanting to make reading fun so that children will love to read. Needless to say, her children's books are meant to be read aloud!